PLA...
OF T...
ROBO...

SCOTT SHIRLEY
AND
SCOTT LISETOR

A PERSPECTIVES BOOK

ORDER DIRECTLY FROM
ANN ARBOR PUBLISHERS
P.O. BOX 1
BELFORD
NORTHUMBERLAND NE70 7JX

Series Editor: Penn Mullin
Cover Design: Damon Rarey
Illustrations: Herb Heidinger

International Standard Book Number: 0-87879-301-1

1 0 9 8
0 9 8 7 6 5

CONTENTS

1 In the Desert................1

2 Escape......................6

3 Lola.......................12

4 Falon......................19

5 Battle 26

6 Victory 32

7 Battle's End 37

8 Over and Out 41

CHAPTER 1

IN THE DESERT

Jon was getting weak very fast. His water supply was gone. He had been in the desert for two days.

Why did I come here, he wondered. He took a sip of water from his canteen.

Jon was an explorer. He worked for a company called *Space, Time, and Place.* His job was to explore strange planets. The company used Jon for the tough jobs. He had become well known. He had been with the company for four years now.

But Jon's new job was not going the way the company had planned. His small spaceship had suddenly lost its power. He didn't know why this had happened. He was forced to land in the desert here on the planet Zare. Jon's company had heard that an enemy was gaining power here. Jon was given the job of finding out what was going on. He was due back home on planet Yola tomorrow. But he'd never make it now.

He was worried. What would people at home think of him now? He was too good a pilot to get stuck in the desert on a small planet like Zare. What did he care about the people here? All that really mattered was being the best pilot and getting well paid for it. But here he was, stuck on the desert. Who could tell how long he would have to stay here? He figured he had about four hours of daylight left.

Jon kept on walking across the desert. Suddenly he stumbled on a rock. He fell forward and landed on his stomach. He was tired. He just stayed on the ground.

Why go on, he thought to himself. Then he heard something. It was the sound of a flying machine. Jon looked up at the sky. A strange machine was headed right at him! At the last minute it turned and landed close to where he was.

Jon stood up and walked toward the machine.

"Who are you? What is your business here?" the pilot yelled as he stepped from the machine.

"My name is Jon Jordan. I am lost and in need of water."

"Silence. You will get water when I want to

give it to you," the pilot said. He pulled a weapon from his machine.

Jon laughed to himself. The pilot held a machine gun like the ones he had seen on Earth One. It was hard to believe someone would still use such an old gun.

"Do you carry a weapon?" the stranger asked.

"No," Jon said as he fired a laser bolt from the hip.

The bolt went through the stranger's shoulder and sliced his arm in two. But he did not seem to feel it. He reached for the fallen machine gun with his other arm.

Jon's second shot cut the stranger in two. He was now harmless but very much alive.

What kind of creature was this stranger? His body lay there in the sand, cut in two. Yet his eyes kept on looking at Jon.

"You'll never get off this planet alive," the stranger said.

"I'm going to give it a good try," Jon answered. He climbed into the stranger's flying machine and prepared to take off.

Jon flew until dark. He could see no sign of life on the planet. He was having a hard time staying awake. Flying was becoming dangerous. When he could no longer stay awake, he found a clearing. He landed the machine and fell asleep instantly.

When Jon woke up, his mouth was very dry. His lips were cracked and bleeding. He had little strength left. He could see a mountain range in the distance. Maybe there was water there. He decided to fly toward it.

He reached the base of a large peak. There he slowed the machine and began to fly upward. He would land when he spotted food and water. About half way up Jon saw something move in the rocks. A small animal sat in a crack It looked like a goat. He stopped his machine, got out, and walked toward the scared animal.

"Sorry, old fellow," Jon said. He raised his gun and killed it.

The animal was skinned within minutes and ready to cook. Jon started a fire. Then he left the camp to look for water. He found a small stream and drank quickly. Then he filled his canteen and headed back to his machine. He cooked the animal he had shot. Then he curled up and was soon asleep.

Slam! It was the noise of a machine gun belt going into position. Jon suddenly woke up. Fifteen guards stood facing him. Each held a gun pointed at his face. They looked like the stranger he had shot the day before.

"Gag and bind him," one guard said. Jon was roughly yanked to his feet. He pushed and pulled against the ropes. He could not get away.

"End his struggle," a guard ordered.

One of the guards swung a club. Jon felt a great pain, then all was darkness.

CHAPTER 2

ESCAPE

Jon's head ached. He awoke in a dark room. He was lying on cold wet stones. It was a cell. But where was this cell? How could he get out?

Jon could see three or four other men around him. Some were asleep. Some were awake. The smell of the place was terrible.

A guard stood at attention on the other side of the bars. Jon wondered if he was human.

"You, lie down." The guard's voice had no feeling as he spoke to Jon.

Jon slowly put his hand into his coat pocket. Good—they had not taken his stars. He pulled out one of them. When it hit something, the star let out electrical forces that destroyed all human tissue.

"I wouldn't try that," said a friendly voice behind Jon. "You can't kill them."

"I know," Jon said. He turned to look at the man who spoke to him.

the small star at him. The second it hit him, the guard's body fell apart.

Jon grabbed his keys and unlocked the door of the cell.

"This is a nice place to visit," Jon said smiling. "But I think I'll take a long vacation. Where is the airport?"

"Good luck," Kang said. "There is a fifty-foot wall around the entire city. The only way out is well guarded. You'll never make it alone. Maybe we could go together."

"No," Jon said. "I work alone."

"Well, thank you for opening the cell. We may meet again," Kang said.

What a strange city, Jon thought as he ran through the streets. So beautiful—and yet, where were the people? There was no one around. Something was very wrong.

He ran until he saw the wall. Kang was right. It was at least fifty feet high. Its smooth sides made it impossible to climb. Jon turned back toward the city. Then he began to search for a place to safely pass the night. He walked up a narrow street. At the end was a small, shabby house. Jon tried the door. Unlocked! He entered softly and looked around. What luck—no one seemed to be at home. Bread and cheese were on

"I wouldn't try that. You can't kill them."

"I am Kang," said the prisoner.

"Kang, I am Jon. Why are you locked in this cell?"

"I am the leader of a group of rebels. This was our city before it was taken over by Falon. He is an evil man, hungry for power."

Jon walked toward the bars and called the guard. When the guard came closer, Jon threw

CHAPTER 3

LOLA

Jon took a great leap out and down. He landed in a perfect roll. Then he was up and running.

The guards stood on the building behind him. One tried the leap, then another. None of them made it to the next building.

Jon watched as they fell ten stories to the ground, then hopped to their feet. He knew they were not humans. But what were they?

He opened the door that led from the roof to the top floor of the building. No guards. It was another empty office building. There must be a place to hide. But maybe there was no need. Jon listened for the sound of guards coming into the building. Then he quietly made his way down the stairs. He expected to hear the guards at any moment. But it was silent. Where are they, he wondered as he opened the door to the street.

Jon saw no guards as he ran through the

12

caused the guard behind him to lose his balance. Both fell down the stairs.

Jon kept going up toward the roof. His legs hurt. He entered the roof through a doorway. The roof was clear, but he could hear footsteps coming up the stairs. It was ten stories down to the street. Jon felt trapped. The next building was at least seven feet away. And worse, it was twelve feet lower. He could hear the guards getting closer. He had to jump.

streets. If he could just keep going until dark, then he could lose them.

Suddenly a guard spotted him. Jon ran to a small courtyard in the center of the city. He hid in the shadows. Then he threw rocks at the guard. The guard ran toward the spot where the rocks had fallen. Then it was easy for Jon to escape unseen. This time he walked quietly away. He found another vacant building and went inside. He quickly bolted the door. At last he could relax!

He had been running for a long time. He had not had time to stop and think. Now he felt safe for the first time in hours. Yet he knew at any moment the guards could break down one of the doors. The guards, he thought. What are they? They cannot be human because they don't die. They must be robots. Someone must control them. How can I find that person, he wondered.

Jon walked to a window and looked out over the deserted city. He could see the high wall around it. Suddenly he heard footsteps. He watched three guards walk by the building where he was hiding. Jon decided to follow them. He climbed to the roof of the building. He could follow the guards by traveling from roof top to roof top. The guards were headed toward the center of the city. Soon he saw them go into a large building.

It seemed to be a safe time for him to get back on the ground. He found the door that led from the roof to the stairway. It was locked! He jumped to another roof and tried that door. It, too, was locked.

Jon jumped back to the last roof he had been on and tried that door to the stairway. It wouldn't open. He was going to have to break a window to get into the building.

He found a heavy stick. Then he leaned over the roof to a window just below. Smash! He waited for the sound of breaking glass to attract one of the guards. No one came, so he slowly lowered himself from the roof through the window. The jagged glass scratched his arms. What's just a scratch or two, he thought. Maybe my troubles are over.

He stood up, and what he saw then stopped him in his tracks. He was staring down the muzzle of a laser pistol. A lovely young woman was holding the pistol. Her face was pale, and she looked scared. But her hand did not shake.

"Move and I'll kill you," she said.

"No problem," Jon said. He raised his arms above his head.

The woman pointed her laser pistol steadily at Jon.

"You are the one my father is after," she said. "Why are you here on planet Zare?"

"My ship crashed here," Jon lied. "And I have been chased ever since I stepped foot on this planet."

"What is your mission? Who sent you here?" the woman asked.

"I told you. I crashed. I didn't plan to stop here."

"Then no one will know if I kill you," she said. Then she calmly raised her gun.

"Wait a minute." Jon could see she meant what she said. "I was sent here. But I was sent only to learn more about your planet. I meant no harm to you or to your people."

"They are not my people. They are his people," said the woman.

"Whose?" Jon asked.

"My father's." There was anger in her voice. "My father and his evil people made them."

"Made them?"

"Yes. They are androids—robots. They are programmed to follow his orders. No matter what the order, they cannot be stopped. Since they are not really alive, they can't die."

"What about all of the people on Zare?" Jon asked.

"All of them are locked in cells. My father had his robots build cells under the buildings all through the city. No one can escape because he had a wall built around the city. His robots guard the cells and the wall."

"Why is he doing this? It sounds as if you don't agree with his actions," Jon said.

The woman looked sad. "Five years ago my father worked as a scientist. He made the first robots to work in our factories. But then he found out that the robots could be used as soldiers. He wanted power. He used the robots to take over the city. Now he wants more power. He is insane! He wants to take over the world. As my father becomes more powerful, he becomes more of a stranger to me. I haven't talked to him face to face in weeks."

"Why not?"

"He has kept me locked up in my rooms under guard. Twice a day he calls me on the closed-circuit television set. I don't think he calls because he really cares about me. He just seems to care if I'm still here."

"You are very beautiful," Jon told the woman. His own words surprised him.

She looked at him. "No one has said anything like that to me in a long time," she said.

"It sounds as if you've been having a very bad time," Jon said softly. "What's your name?"

"Lola," she answered and lowered her gun. She dropped her gun to her side. "And I'm so tired."

"Let me be your friend," Jon said. "Maybe we can help one another."

Lola smiled at him. "A friend—I don't have many of those left."

"What about family?" asked Jon.

"There's no one," said Lola sadly. "My mother died when I was just a child. My brother was killed by invaders from another planet. That's when my father changed. That's why he doesn't trust anyone."

Jon felt sorry for this sad, tired young woman. He tried to think of something to say to make her feel better. But no words came.

Suddenly they heard three loud slams at the door. "Your gun!" screamed Jon.

"Lola!" voices yelled from outside the door. "Do not let him escape."

"You must go now," Lola whispered. Her voice sounded worried. "If they know I helped you to escape they will put me in a cell."

Jon took one last look at Lola. Then he jumped back to the roof he had come from. When he looked back, he could see three guards bursting into Lola's room. One of them grabbed her. He pulled her through the doorway. The other two guards were looking out the window.

Jon ran, but he promised himself to return and save Lola.

CHAPTER 4

FALON

Jon suddenly realized he had not eaten all day. His stomach ached with hunger. It was getting dark. He had been on the roof for about an hour. He was sure now that all the guards were in the large building in town. They were there to guard Lola. Now would be the perfect time to escape. But how was he to get down to the street?

Jon walked to the edge of the building. He hoped to be able to find a way down. A drain pipe was sticking up over the top of the roof. He tested the pipe. It seemed firm. He lowered himself over the side of the building. Was he crazy to trust his life to that thin piece of pipe? Seven stories was a long way to fall. But the piece of pipe held. He made it down safely. Then he set off down the street.

Jon's eyes and ears were alert for any sights or sounds. Suddenly he heard footsteps ahead. He ducked into a small doorway. Then he pushed himself back against the door. He hardly dared to breathe.

Suddenly the door swung inward. Jon was thrown backward into the room. The door shut instantly. Silence followed. A light flared a moment later. Jon looked around. Standing in front of him was his former cellmate, Kang.

"Kang! How did you get here?" Jon cried.

"No time to tell you now. Where's Lola?" Kang asked.

Jon told Kang about his meeting with Lola. "They've got her, but I don't know where," he said.

"Poor girl," said Kang. "I've known her since she was a child. Her life has not been an easy one."

"Do you know her father?" asked Jon.

Kang looked sad. "Yes, I do. He's mad, and he must be stopped."

"Will he hurt Lola?" Jon asked.

"He'll hurt anyone who gets in his way," Kang told him. "We've got to rescue her. Now! There's no time to waste."

Suddenly Jon and Kang felt that another body was in the room. Jon reached into his pocket and pulled out a star. He threw it toward the pair of eyes glowing in the shadows. The star hit the creature directly between the eyes. As it fell, the creature let out a scream. Jon could see it was one of the guards.

"That was a close one, buddy," Jon said. He looked at the space where Kang had stood just seconds before.

"Kang," yelled Jon. But there was no answer. The room was empty.

Jon stood still. He had to think. He walked toward the door. Then he stumbled over Kang's bag. It was full of food. "I know Kang wouldn't mind," Jon told himself as he ate hungrily. The bread, fruit, and nuts tasted wonderful. When he had finished, Jon ran out into the street. Then he ran toward the building where he was sure Lola was being held. He had no trouble getting into the building. But would he ever be able to find Lola inside? He ran up the stairs two at a time. He peered into an empty hallway. Then he started down it. Suddenly he saw two guards.

Jon ducked as the guards fired. Then he turned and ran up the stairs. The guards chased after him. He quickly turned and grabbed the barrel of one of the guard's guns. He swung the guard around, slamming him into his partner. Both guns went crashing to the floor.

The guards were almost helpless without their guns. Jon shoved one guard out the window. He spun around in time to send the other one crashing into the far wall. Then the guard tried to stand up. He stared at Jon with dead-looking eyes. Jon ran down the stairs. He found an open door and went into a large room. On the far wall was an empty elevator shaft. Jon ran to the shaft and grabbed the cable. The cable was slippery. Jon began to slide down it. He could feel himself falling.

Suddenly he spotted a ladder on the wall of the shaft. Not a minute to lose! He jumped from the cable and grabbed it. He felt like screaming. He was in terrible pain. His arms had been jerked hard by the sudden stop. Now they felt like jelly.

Climbing to the bottom was pure torture for Jon. Finally he reached it. Then he sat down for a moment and rubbed his aching arms.

When he could stand the pain, Jon stepped out from the shaft. Ahead was an empty hallway without doors or windows. He ran down the hall and turned a corner. Then he rushed toward the door ahead. He opened it a crack and looked through.

Twelve guards with machine guns stood silently. A circle of cells surrounded them. Lola sat

The cable was slippery. Jon began to slide down.

alone on a cot in one of the cells. Kang was in the next cell.

Jon shut the door quickly. He had noticed an opening for air on the ceiling of the guards' room. Then he had an idea. He had seen an air opening back in the elevator shaft. He climbed up to the ladder. Then he went into the opening. He soon reached the place that overlooked the guards. Then Jon heard voices below. He saw Falon enter and walk up to Lola's cell.

"How can you do this to your own daughter?" Lola was saying.

From his hiding place Jon saw Falon, Lola's father, for the first time. He was a huge man with dark, cruel eyes.

"Be still, child," Falon's voice was cold. "You have betrayed me. You helped the prisoner escape. You are no longer my daughter. You must die!"

"Swine!" The voice shocked Jon. It was Kang.

"You will die also, Kang," Falon said.

Poor Lola, Jon thought. She has not seen her father in weeks. Now he sends her to death!

Jon couldn't hold himself back another second. He pulled a piece of pipe from the airduct and jumped right down on Falon. Jon knocked the older man off his feet and stood over him. He raised the pipe over Falon's head.

"Your guards will drop their weapons or this pipe will crush your skull. My hand is quicker than their bullets," Jon said. He jumped back as if to bring down the pipe.

"Drop your weapons and leave," Falon said to the guards. Sweat poured from his forehead.

"Release the prisoners," Jon ordered.

Since he had no guards left, Falon was forced to carry out the order himself. He opened his daughter's cell first, then Kang's.

"Falon's guards will come back," Lola said to Jon. "Quick, help me with the main switches. We'll free all of the prisoners in the city."

Jon rushed forward as the first group of guards came back through the door. Kang and Lola were behind him. It was too late to hit the switch. Two guards pushed them against the wall. Were they going to die here just minutes away from freedom?

CHAPTER 5

BATTLE

Jon knew he had to act fast. He took a swing at one guard, then another. But it was a never-ending battle. As soon as he knocked down one guard, another one appeared.

"Oh, no! The robot swordsmen," Lola cried. Fear was in her eyes.

Jon turned to see four guards with swords headed his way.

"Grab the swords. It's our only hope," Kang yelled. He had managed to get free from his guards.

"Jon, watch it!" A swordsman was about to stick his weapon into Jon's back. Kang grabbed the sword just in time. Jon was fighting still another swordsman. He managed to grab a weapon away from this one.

"Go for their heads," yelled Lola. She fought to free herself from two guards.

Jon stuck his sword between one of the swordsmen's eyes. He fell to the ground useless.

"Well, we finally found a way to stop them," Jon said to Kang. The two men were side by side fighting off the swordsmen. With each swing of the sword at least two swordsmen would fall.

Free for a moment, Lola was suddenly grabbed by one of the swordsmen.

She gave him a swift kick in the stomach and sent him falling backward. This time Lola ran toward the control panel. She hoped to get to the main switch, which would release the prisoners. But the guards must have known what she planned. Six of them stood between her and the panel.

Kang and Jon were still fighting the swordsmen. At least ten unarmed guards lay useless on the floor now. And no more swordsmen had appeared.

Lola needed a weapon in order to get to the control panel. She remembered the loaded laser her father kept in a cabinet. It was in the room behind the elevator shaft. If I'm quick and lucky, I'll get there, she thought.

She ran toward the room faster than she had ever known she could move. She pulled open the cabinet and reached inside. The cool metal of the laser gun felt good to her hand. It felt even better as she fired it at the robots' heads. One by one they toppled to the floor.

This time nothing was going to stop her from pulling the switch.

Meanwhile, Jon and Kang kept battling the swordsmen. But each swordsman that fell was instantly replaced by another!

"Swish, swish." There was no mistaking the sound. It was Lola's laser gun. She had come back to help Jon and Kang. But first she had pulled the switch to free all the prisoners.

Lola's aim was perfect. She calmly fired the laser at guard after guard. But she had to be very careful that she didn't hit her two friends as she fired.

Suddenly Jon saw a horrible looking creature coming towards Lola! It was at least seven feet tall. And Jon could see right through its huge body!

"Behind you!" Jon yelled to warn Lola.

Lola kept firing her laser at the creature's horrible scaley head. But the laser had no effect on the creature. He kept on coming toward her.

"I'll take this one," Kang cried. He threw his body on top of the creature.

Lola downed another swordsman with her

Jon saw a horrible-looking creature.

laser. Then she grabbed his weapon. She ran over to Kang. He was doing hand-to-hand battle with the creature.

Jon had just flattened the last swordsman. He ran over to help Kang.

Now Kang was on top of the creature. He used strength he didn't know he had to hold the creature on the ground.

"Lola, hold onto the laser and give me the swords," Jon said. He grabbed the sword Kang had dropped. "Keep firing to keep the guards away. Kang and I will bring this big guy down for good."

"Try using the swords," Lola said between laser shots.

She knew her father liked to make androids that could destroy one another. She had never seen this creature before. Why had her father created him?

Jon stuck the first sword into the creature's left leg. The huge body fell to the ground. A second sword went through the creature's stomach, and he was down for good.

Lola, Jon, and Kang quickly headed for the stairs. Guards littered the floor behind them. As they reached the first landing, they heard footsteps coming toward them.

"More guards?" Jon asked.

He and Kang were ready with their swords. Lola held the laser ready to fire.

"Hold your fire," said a voice ahead of them.

It was one of the former prisoners. He led a large group that looked ready to fight.

"What's it like out on the street?" Kang asked.

"Listen," the stranger said.

The air was filled with the sound of shouting voices.

"We are looking for guards," the stranger continued. "We're going to fill up all the cells with guards."

"We got rid of most of the guards," Jon told him. "But we left a few for you to lock up."

"Hurry. Our people are free. There is much to do," Kang said.

He threw open the door to the street. The sight in front of him was not a happy one.

CHAPTER 6

VICTORY

Robot soldiers were everywhere. They were battling the newly-released prisoners. More and more robots were filling the streets.

"The factory. My father must be at the factory," Lola called to Jon and Kang. "He has thousands of these robots all ready to take over if the old ones are destroyed."

"Now I understand why there are so many of them," Jon said.

Lola, Jon, and Kang ran toward the factory. Machine gun fire crackled around them. It broke windows and bounced off the street. The noise was terrifying.

"We're almost there," Lola said, running between the two men.

"What's that?" Jon asked, looking up at the sky.

A spaceship hovered overhead. It was full of

guards. And one had a machine gun pointed in their direction.

Lola handed her sword to Kang. Raising her laser, she fired at the guards in the spaceship. The front panel of the spaceship burst into flames. It became a cloud of fire and metal. But the guards fell through the air, landed on their feet, and kept on fighting. Lola soon finished them off with her laser.

"Let's get going before they send more spaceships after us," Kang said.

The three ran through the streets. Then Lola directed them through an alley. She motioned for them to stop.

"That's my father's factory," she said pointing across the street.

Jon couldn't believe what he saw. Hundreds of guards surrounded the factory.

"Stay back or they will see us," he whispered to his friends.

"We'll never get past those guards," Kang said.

"If we don't, my father will continue to put out more guards," Lola said. "How much longer do you think our people can fight?"

"We have no choice but to destroy the factory," Jon said.

"But how?" Lola asked.

"See that spaceship over there? It's going to blow the building up," Jon said. "Lola, cover me with the laser."

Jon ran the 100 yards to the spaceship. Lola's aim was perfect. She got rid of every guard in Jon's path.

Jon opened the engine compartment of the spaceship. He reached in and turned the energy switch to overload. The engine would blow up in thirty seconds, so he had to move very quickly. He ran to the control panel, then he set it at ninety miles an hour on automatic pilot.

"Stand back," Jon yelled as he released the brake.

The empty spaceship shot forward. It reached ninety miles an hour almost instantly. Then it shot through the crowd of guards. It sent them flying in all directions. Finally it smashed through the wall of the factory. The sound of the explosion was deafening.

Jon ran to where Kang and Lola had taken cover. They watched as the factory fell. It was now just a pile of wood and stones. There would be no more robots.

"We have stopped Falon," Kang said proudly.

But there were tears in Lola's eyes. Jon put his arms around her.

Finally it smashed through the wall of the factory. The sound of the explosion was deafening.

"My father wasn't always evil," Lola said. Jon held her closer.

"You are very brave," Kang said. "You sacrificed your father so your people could be free once again."

The three had been so busy with their own adventure that they missed what was going on in the city. The battle was over. The air was filled with shouts of joy.

Kang ran through the streets yelling, "We are free, free, free!"

CHAPTER 7

BATTLE'S END

"No. It is not possible for me to stay here. I am an explorer," Jon told Kang and Lola.

The three friends were back in the room where Lola had been held prisoner by the guards.

Lola and Kang had been trying to get Jon to stay on Zare and help them rebuild the city.

"We need you because you are an explorer," Kang told Jon. "This is a large planet. Most of it has not been explored. After the city is rebuilt, we must build more cities. Then we will see what is beyond the desert."

"And you are a hero to our people," Lola said to Jon. "You are the leader we need. You have brought peace and hope."

Why had this happened, Jon wondered. He had been on hundreds of missions since going to work for *Space, Time, and Place*. Never before had he worried about people on any of the planets.

And right now Jon was also worried about his job. The agency had expected him back at headquarters with a report about the planet. He was three days overdue. He had to get back. His small spaceship was somewhere out in the desert. The power loss that had forced him to land was probably caused by Falon. If he could just get to his ship and take off!

"Please, my friends," Jon said to Lola and Kang. "help me get to my spaceship."

"OK. But I hate to have you leave us," Lola said, smiling. "So much has happened in the past few days."

It was difficult for Jon not to look Lola in the eye. But he knew if he did, he could never say no to her. His feelings for her were already mixing him up.

Kang was holding open the door to the street. For the first time Jon could walk without having to fight or hide.

The people in the streets were walking in a daze. The useless pieces of robots were everywhere.

"You two must lead the people," Jon said to Lola and Kang.

"But they know I am Falon's daughter," Lola said. "They will not trust me."

"The people know you were held prisoner," Kang answered. "They know you did not agree with your father's evil ways."

"Lola, oh, Lola!" A young woman was running toward Lola. "I'm so glad you are all right. We have been so worried about you," Lola's friend said as they hugged each other.

"Jon, Kang, this is my friend Tasha."

"Lola, did you know the factory was blown up? The people believe your father was inside," Tasha said.

"Do you know what caused the factory to blow up?" Lola asked.

"No," said Tasha. "No one knows."

"This is your hero," Jon said. He grabbed Kang by the shoulder.

"You, Kang? You destroyed the factory?" Tasha asked. She was jumping up and down shouting, "Kang! Kang! Kang is our hero."

Others joined in the cheering. "Kang! Kang! Long live Kang!" the people shouted.

A large crowd was gathering. Kang was at the center.

Jon grabbed Lola's hand. He pulled her away from the crowd.

"Help me find a spaceship, Lola," Jon said. "I have to get out to the desert and find my own ship. Please, Lola."

"How can I say no to you? You have done so much for me and for my people. I'll fly you wherever you want," Lola answered.

CHAPTER 8

OVER AND OUT

Lola and Jon had been in the air for more than an hour when Jon spotted his ship.

"There she is. Right where I left her."

Lola brought the spaceship down without a bump.

"You do want me to wait to see if your ship starts," Lola said. She was trying to joke. But it was difficult. And saying goodbye to Jon was going to be very hard.

"Lola, it isn't going to be easy for me to leave. I care a lot about you and Kang and your people. But, like you and Kang, I have a job to do," Jon told Lola as they climbed down from the spaceship.

"In a way I hope it won't start," Lola said as they walked toward Jon's ship.

"That's just how I feel!" Jon thought to himself.

Jon opened the door to the ship.

"How long will it take you to get home?" Lola asked.

"It was a twelve-hour ride here." Jon was adjusting the dials on the control panel. Lola stood next to the ship. She talked to him through the open door.

"It seems to be working. Now I'll try the radio. Mission control, come in mission control. This is Jon."

"Jon, this is mission control. You're three days overdue. You better have a good excuse. If you were just goofing off..."

"Mission control, you can expect me in about twelve hours. So long. Over and out."

Lola had stood by silently while Jon talked on the radio.

"Well, I guess this is it," she said. "I'd sure like to see a copy of your report." She was trying to sound happy.

"Lola, you are a dear friend." Jon had made the mistake of looking Lola straight in the eye. "I am going back because I have a job to finish."

"I know," Lola said sadly. "We both have things we must do. But how I wish you would remain here on Zare with Kang and me."

"I hope to be able to return soon. Would you

let me help you and your people rebuild the city?"

"Will you really return, Jon?"

"I shall."

"Soon?"

"I promise," Jon told her.

"Will you really return, Jon?"
"I promise," Jon told her.

Lola kissed Jon on the cheek. Then she stepped away from the ship. She headed back toward her own spaceship.

Jon started the engine of his ship. He watched Lola walking away across the sand. How he wished he could stay with her and help rebuild the city *now*. But he would come back. He was sure of that. There was so much to come back for. He waved to Lola and got his ship ready for takeoff.